D1111906

Madeleine

(ET NUNC MANET IN TE)

Betty L. Plum

Madeleine

(ET NUNC MANET IN TE)

ANDRÉ GIDE

TRANSLATED FROM THE FRENCH,

WITH AN INTRODUCTION AND NOTES, BY

Justin O'Brien

ELEPHANT PAPERBACKS
Ivan R. Dee, Inc., Publisher, Chicago

First ELEPHANT PAPERBACK edition published 1989 by Ivan R. Dee, Inc., 1332 North Halsted Street, Chicago 60622. Manufactured in the United States of America.

Library of Congress Cataloging-in-Publication Data
Gide, André, 1869–1951.
  [Nunc Manet in Te. English]
  Madeleine = Et Nunc Manet in Te / André Gide: Translated from the French, with an introduction and notes, by Justin O'Brien.—1st Elephant Paperback ed.
  Reprint. Originally published: New York: Knopf, 1952.
  1. Gide, André, 1869–1951—Biography—Marriage. 2. Gide, Madeleine Louise Mathilde, ca. 1867–1938. 3. Authors, French—20th century—Biography—Marriage. 4. Authors' wives—France—Biography. I. Title. II. Title: Nunc Manet in Te.
PQ2613.I2Z523   1989   848'.91209   89-35479
ISBN 0-929587-19-7

INTRODUCTION

BY

JUSTIN O'BRIEN

Rarely has a writer confessed himself more intimately in public than André Gide. His vast *Journals*, covering the sixty years of his literary life, and especially his frank memoirs, known in English as *If It Die . . .* , presented as sincere an image of himself as he could paint. To such documents he added *Corydon*, his plea for homosexuality, as explicit expression of the constant need for self-justification that, directly or by implication, brought his own anomaly into so many of his works of imagination. Having no confidence in posthumous publications and fearing the zeal of parents and friends for "camouflaging the dead," he long ago stated his belief that "it is better to be hated for what one is than loved for what one is not."

Yet, even to those who had studied his work most attentively, the entire chapter of his conjugal life remained a mystery. Years after Mme André Gide's death on 17 April 1938, the most enlightened commentators did not even know her real given name and had to call her by the symbolic name Emmanuèle, which Gide had consistently given her in his writings. Until today, no photograph or portrait of her has ever been published to place beside the myriad images of her photogenic husband. No indiscreet friend, so long as André Gide lived, provided impressions of her in print with which to fill out the muted sketch emerging from Gide's discreet prose.

The memoirs furnish the largest number of trustworthy details about "Emmanuèle." There we first see her and her two younger sisters spending the summers at their father's estate of Cuverville near the Norman coast, where their little cousin André shared their games and studies. In the beginning she was too quiet for his taste, always quitting the noisy games for a book, forever yielding her turn or her share with smiling grace. As the years passed, he came to prefer her for that very reserve and gravity, and finally, when he was about twelve and she fourteen, occurred the startling event that suddenly revealed her secret sadness and gave his life a new orientation. For, upon realizing how the discovery of her mother's adultery had struck the child with unbearable grief, he decided at once to devote his life to her happiness. "I hid in the depths of my heart the secret of my destiny," he later wrote. "Had it been less contradicted and crossed, I should not be writing these memoirs."

From this point onward, his cousin was to be in his thoughts constantly. She was, indeed, the dominant influence of his adolescent years, open to such varied influences. Each step in his intellectual and spiritual development had to be taken, not only in full view of her, but even in unison with her. While reading, he would write her initials opposite every sentence that he wanted to share with her. Away from her, he wrote her innumerable letters, which later struck him as odiously artificial.

Thus what André Gide always maintained was the only love of his life began in childhood. When her father died, in 1890, Madeleine Rondeaux (as we now know her real name to have been) became the responsibility of her aunts, and particularly of the widowed Mme Paul Gide. Although he was not yet twenty-one and she was his first cousin, young André already planned to marry Madeleine. The following year his first published work, *Les Cahiers d'André Walter*, crystalized that youthful love and constituted, at least in the author's mind, a bid for her hand. Made up in part of extracts from his actual diary kept during his seventeenth and eighteenth years, it depicts a pure, intellectualized love rather like that of Dante for Beatrice, divorced of the carnal, impossible of fulfillment, and in any case thwarted by Emmanuèle's marriage to another. By making his hero succumb to madness as a result of losing his beloved, the writer hoped to convince his family of the intensity of his love. But with its frank recognition of the body's demands and its typically adolescent insistence upon the necessity of dissociating the spiritual and the physical, the book formed a disturbing document from the hand of so austere a youth brought up in the strictest Calvinist tradition. That Madeleine never told her cousin what she thought of his work and rejected the proposal that followed its publication is not altogether surprising.

Two years later, in the autumn of 1893, came the great turning-point in André Gide's life when, in Tunisia during his first extensive journey from home, he first indulged in pederasty. At the same time that he thus discovered his anomaly, a serious illness and long convalescence taught him the value of a life of sensation, so that he returned to France in the summer of 1894 a different man. In the total change he had undergone, the precise orientation of his sexual impulse, which he could neither believe nor accept, doubtless seemed but one manifestation of a general awakening. So changed was he, indeed, that of the former self there remained only his literary vocation and his ethereal love for Madeleine Rondeaux.

Another sojourn in North Africa the following winter and a decisive encounter with Oscar Wilde on the eve of his scandalous trial must have contributed greatly to Gide's self-knowledge. But his recall to Paris in the spring of 1895 and particularly his mother's death at the end of May suddenly stifled the new man in him. The systole-diastole of his young life, outwardly figured by the lure of an exotic Africa and the attachment to a sheltering home, was brusquely interrupted. Years later he wrote in his memoirs: "That very freedom for which I panted, while my mother was still alive, stunned and choked me like a gush of fresh air, perhaps even frightened me. Like the prisoner abruptly set free, I felt dizzy—like the kite with its string suddenly cut, like the boat cast adrift, like the derelict about to be tossed by the wind and the waves."

The one fixed point in his life remained his deep affection for his slightly older cousin. As family concern about his way of life grew during his early literary career and his first trips to Africa, the relatives in general had gradually come to look upon his eventual marriage with Madeleine as a possible steadying influence. While doubting that such a union would be happy, his uncle Charles Gide (not yet the internationally famous economist he was to become) had written the youth's mother with a scholar's instinctive caution: "Yet, if it does not take place, probably both of them will be surely unhappy, so that there remains only a choice between a certain evil and a possible one." Finally, during their last hours together, Mme Gide, foreseeing her death and perhaps fearing to leave him alone, had admitted to her son that she wished him to marry the niece whom she had long considered as her daughter-in-law.

André himself was convinced that his cousin needed him to be happy, and when, shortly after his loss, he asked for her hand he was thinking less of himself, he asserts, than of her. Intoxicated by the sublime, he was ready to give himself away as he had just distributed among indifferent relatives the jewels and mementos belonging to his mother. As the mature Gide says most meaningfully in the last lines of his memoirs: "Our most sincere acts are also the least calculated; the explanation one looks for later on is useless. Fate was leading me, perhaps also a secret need to challenge my nature; for was it not virtue itself that I loved in her? It was heaven that my insatiable hell was marrying; but at the moment I was omitting that hell; the tears of my grief had extinguished all its fires; I was as if dazzled with azure, and what I refused to see had ceased to exist for me. I believed that I could give myself to her wholly, and I did so without withholding anything."

On 8 October 1895 the young cousins were married at Étretat, a few miles from Madeleine's estate of Cuverville, with a Protestant minister from Rouen, named Roberty, officiating; the best man was Élie Allégret, himself a minister and missionary, who later became director of all French Protestant missions.

The very conception of a "marriage of Heaven and Hell" (which must have been suggested to Gide by his translation in 1922 of William Blake's prophetic work with that title) already divulges much of the truth while surely explaining the name that Gide consistently gave his wife in his writings. He might have satisfied her natural discretion and fear of the limelight by adopting one of the unused given names of Louise-Mathilde-Madeleine Rondeaux. It would be quite unlike Gide ever to have explained, yet it is strange that no one else has ever pointed out, that the name Emmanuel is interpreted in the Bible as "God with us." Throughout life his wife appeared to André Gide as his refuge, his anchor to windward, his link with tradition and the past, his protection against everything in himself that he feared, and his possible salvation. It is for this reason that her simple headstone in the little cemetery at Cuver-ville-en-Caux bears a verse from the beatitudes: "Blessed are the peacemakers: for they shall be called the children of God." In the French version of Ostervald, which Gide chose for the stone-carver, the wording is even more appropriate, for it reads: "*Heureux ceux qui procurent la paix . . .*"

Immediately after the marriage, the young couple set out on a protracted journey that was to last until May of the following year. After two months in Switzerland and another two in Italy, they reached North Africa in February 1896; there they visited Tunis, El Kantara, Biskra, and Toug-gourt. This was André Gide's third sojourn in the desert and its oases; it seems as if a fatal attraction, which he will later attribute to the Michel of his *Immoralist,* drew him back to the scene of his awakening. From Neuchâtel a fortnight after the wedding, he wrote to a friend: "Now I am beginning an indefatigable rest beside the calmest of wives." But only three months later he wrote from Rome: "Here it is madly beautiful weather and my senses and soul are stampeding; I am drinking in the sunlight like an over-warm wine and my wisdom is confounded." The systolic rhythm was re-established.

Instead of tying him down to Paris and the two Norman estates that he and his wife had now inherited, marriage was not to influence his restless roving—as his next and seventh work, with its praise of the nomadic state, was to prove. But Madeleine could not have felt the same interest in Africa as he did. It was not long, in fact, before she renounced accompanying her husband on his many travels and settled into the retired life to which she was faithful until her death in 1938 at the age of seventy-one.

That life centered in the château of Cuverville, in which she had grown up. The long three-story house with its fourteen master bedrooms dates from the eighteenth century, of which it has the typical mansard roof and small-paned windows. The pale yellow, white-shuttered dwelling is ornamented solely by the precision of its proportions and its central pediment, bright against the slate roof. It stands in a seventeen-acre park surrounded by over three hundred acres of farmlands. In front of the stone steps extends a vast lawn shaded by a giant cedar planted one hundred years ago by the grandfather. On the left runs an avenue of tall beeches. Behind the house, protected by a thick curtain of trees, a flower-garden basks in the sun, its winding paths outlined by espalier fruit-trees. As is customary in such houses, the common rooms extend from front to back, receiving light from windows at both ends; both façades

command a broad view of the wild, monotonous
landscape of the Caux region, intersected by beech
groves for shelter against the Channel winds.

Gide's love for Cuverville is apparent from
many descriptions in his work, such as that of
Fongueusemare in *Strait Is the Gate*; but perhaps
the most evocative one occurs in his *Journals* for
May 1906: "The grass of the lawn is deep like the
grass in a churchyard. Each apple tree in the farm-
yard is a thick mass of blossoms. The whitewashed
trunks prolong their whiteness right down to the
ground. Every breath of air brings me some per-
fume, especially that of the wistaria, on the left,
against the house, so loaded with blossoms that
one can hear its bees from here. . . . Yesterday
before sunset I had just time to visit the garden
thoroughly. The big apple tree leaning toward
the tennis court, smiling and rustling in the last
rays of the sun, was becoming pink. A frightful
shower, a few hours before, had submerged the
countryside and purged the sky of all clouds.

Every bit of foliage was brimming as with tears, particularly that of the two big copper beeches, not yet copper-colored, but transparent and blond, which fell about me like soft hair. When, going out by the little door in the bottom of the garden, I saw the sun again and the luminous cliff in front of it formed by the grove of beeches, everything struck me as so affectionately beautiful, so new, that I could have wept with joy."

The interior of the large dwelling possesses the same charm as the sober exterior. On the right of the entrance hall, one enters a white-paneled drawing-room with windows at both ends. Its mahogany furniture and petit-point armchairs harmonize with the gay draperies and honey-colored parquet floor. On the left of the hall opens the dining-room, with its three wicker armchairs by the wood fire, each sheltering a majestic Siamese cat. Meals are served with an Anglo-Saxon simplicity at a round table by one of the windows. Near the table a door leads to Mme Gide's domain:

the pantry, milk-room, storeroom, and vast kitchen with its gleaming coppers. "There Mme Gide spends hours at her daily tasks in a stifling odor of kerosene, wax, and turpentine. For the religion of polish reigns at Cuverville. Everything that can be rubbed shines like a mirror," writes Roger Martin du Gard; and, faithful to the technique of his *World of the Thibaults*, he gives a striking example: "The staircase is a model of its kind: according to an unalterable rite at least fifty years old, every morning patient servants with wool cloths tirelessly caress all its surfaces, all its flat spaces, all its reliefs—from the red tiles of the steps and their oak borders to the least projections of the iron balustrade. As an alluvium of several generations, a thick layer of hardened wax, transparent like a topaze-colored varnish, makes the whole staircase look as if carved out of some precious, polished, indefinable material, a block of dark amber."

This was the world of Madeleine André Gide,

within which she willingly circumscribed her life. In summers, and often at other times of the year, she was surrounded by her sisters Jeanne and Valentine—the former married to Professor Marcel Drouin, and the latter the widow of Marcel Gilbert—and their children. Her best friend, Agnès Copeau, the wife of the great theatrical director, frequently came with her children also. Mme Gide hardly lived at all in the rambling house that André Gide had built in Auteuil and never learned to like; there is no evidence that she ever set foot in the rue Vaneau apartment that became his Paris headquarters in 1928 and where he died in 1951.

In the last years of Gide's life the rumor circulated that he had an illegitimate daughter who had grown up in the south of France. Reference to the *Journals* showed frequent mention, from 1926 on, of "little Catherine." After the war she began to be seen in his company—an attractive young woman with a marked resemblance to her father. By the time of the Nobel Prize, their photograph had appeared in newspapers, and the writer was known to be a grandfather. In the ensuing years the date of Catherine Gide's birth has been given as 1923 and her mother has been several times identified in print as Élisabeth Van Rysselberghe, the daughter of the painter Théo Van Rysselberghe.

So much could be gleaned during Gide's lifetime. By implication one got the impression that the poet Francis Jammes summarized when he referred to his friend's wife as "Madame Sainte Gide." Nonetheless, the intimate drama of Gide's conjugal life remained a mystery, as did the personality of the wife who had never shared his fame.

With what keen curiosity and excited anticipation, then, did we note a passage in the last *Journals* in which Gide, blocked in German-occupied Tunis in March 1943, wondered if he would ever see again the private papers he had left in Paris— among which, he says, "the manuscript relating to

Em., in which I had transcribed the unpublished parts of my *Journal* and everything concerning that supreme part of my life which might explain and throw light upon it." On his return to Paris he found the precious documents intact and was thus able to have them printed in Neuchâtel by his friend Richard Heyd under the strange title of *Et nunc manet in te*, in a private edition of but thirteen copies, each bearing the name of the recipient. That was in 1947 at the time of his receiving the Nobel Prize. But even then, to all but a handful of most intimate friends, the bibliographical entry of a new Latin title for the year 1947 remained a tantalizing mystery until a few months after Gide's death, when, according to the author's wishes, M. Heyd issued the text publicly. The present translation, with annotations added as for the American and English editions of the *Journals*, has been made from that publication of 1951.

Now we *know*. At last all our questions are answered—as well as it was in André Gide's power to answer them, and in a prose as vibrant as anything he ever wrote. In this letter to his dead wife, which he could never have addressed to her in her lifetime, the ring of sincerity is unmistakable. At once self-accusatory and self-excusing, it fully presents the husband's side of the case. As for her whose life was sacrificed to the cruel needs of genius, we now know that she was forever unable and unwilling to defend herself. As Roger Martin du Gard noted at the time of her death (but published only in 1951): "She left nothing in writing, no intimate note, no message for him. No one will ever know precisely what a cross she bore, what she grasped, what she suspected, what she refused to know, what she knew despite herself, what she forgave or did not forgive. She carried her secrets with her."

Yet now we are able to grasp the tragedy of

xxiii

André Gide's life and to recognize, as we had suspected, that his wife stood at the very heart of his
life and work.

CONTENTS

Madeleine

(ET NUNC MANET IN TE)

. . . et nunc manet in te.

VIRGIL (Culex) [1]

Yesterday evening I was thinking of her; I was talking with her, as I often used to do, more easily in imagination than in her presence; when suddenly I said to myself: but she is dead. . . .

To be sure, I often happened to spend long successions of days away from her; but in childhood I had got into the habit of bringing back to her the harvest of my day and of mentally associating her with my sorrows and joys. This is what I was doing yesterday evening, when suddenly I remembered that she was dead.

At once everything lost its color, everything clouded over—both these recent recollections of

---

[1] Line 269 of *The Culex* or *The Gnat*, a poem of doubtful authorship often attributed to Virgil's youth. André Gide interpreted these words as suggesting that now his wife lived on solely in his memory.

3

a time spent far from her and this very moment when I was recalling them, for I was reliving them in thought only for her. I immediately realized that, having lost her, I had ceased to have a *raison d'être* and I no longer knew why I was going on living.

I never much liked that name Emmanuèle which I gave her in my writings out of regard for her reticence.[2] Perhaps I liked her real name only because, from my childhood on, it evoked all she represented for me of grace, sweetness, intelligence, and kindness. It seemed to me usurped when borne by another; she alone, it seemed to me, had a right to it. When, for my *Porte étroite,* I invented the name of Alissa, I did not do so out of affectation but through reserve. There must be only one Alissa.

[2] Madeleine Rondeaux, who became Mme André Gide in 1895 and died in April 1938, always appeared in her husband's writings as Emmanuèle.

4

But the Alissa of my book was not she. It was not her portrait that I drew. She served me merely as a starting-point for my heroine, and I do not think she recognized herself much in Alissa. She never said anything to me of my book, so that I can only guess at the thoughts she may have had as she read it. Those thoughts are painful to me, like everything that resulted from that profound sorrow which I began to suspect only much later, for her extreme reserve kept her from letting it be seen, and from talking of it.

Did not the drama I had imagined for my book, however beautiful it may have been, prove to her that I was blind to the real drama? How much simpler than Alissa, more normal and more *ordinary* (I mean less like a Corneille heroine, and less tense) must she have felt herself to be? For she constantly doubted herself, her beauty, her virtues, everything that constituted her personality and charm. I believe that, late in life, I managed to understand her much better; but at

5

the height of my love how greatly I was mistaken about her! For the whole effort of my love tended less to bridge the gap between us than to bridge the gap between her and that ideal figure I invented. At least this is the way it strikes me today; and I do not think Dante acted differently with Beatrice. It is partly, it is especially through a need for making amends that I am trying, now that she is gone, to recover the trace of what she was. I should not like the ghost of Alissa to obscure the person she really was.

Madeleine had vigorously insisted that I not try to see her sister [8] on her deathbed. On my return from Senegal I had learned that at last, after two months of frightful suffering, Valentine had just attained the only repose she could still hope for. I planned to hasten at once to the house of the deceased, where my two nieces were expecting

[8] Valentine Rondeaux, who became Mme Marcel Gilbert, died in March 1938.

me; by telegraph and then by telephone Madeleine begged me not to do so: "I beg you urgently not to go to rue de l'Éperon before having seen me." Since nothing else kept me in Paris, where no one was yet informed of my return, I took the first train for Cuverville.[4] And when I asked her the reason for her insistence, she said: "It was painful for me to think that you would see Valentine's beautiful face distorted by her suffering. I have been told that she was disfigured. That is not the memory I want you to have of her." I recognized in this her instinctive turning away from any painful sight. But the reasons she gave me seemed to me to hold only for her. By putting myself in her place I managed to understand them; I could not share them. Nonetheless, I recalled what she had said to me that day—that is, a month earlier—and on the point of opening the door of her little

---

4 Cuverville-en-Caux, about fifteen miles northeast of Le Havre, was the site of the estate Madeleine Rondeaux inherited from her father, where she spent most of her married life.

room at Cuverville, where the news of her death had suddenly recalled me—where Yvonne de Lestrange,[5] at whose house at Chitré I had been tarrying, had brought me by car and left me—yes, on the point of opening the door of that room now inhabited only by her dead body, I hesitated, wondering if she would not have said to me likewise: "Do not try to see me again." Then I thought that, since she had undergone almost no agony, I should find her almost as I had left her a fortnight earlier, simply soothed by death.

When I approached the bed where she was lying, I was surprised by the gravity of her face. It seemed as if the grace and amenity that radiated from her kindness had lived altogether in her eyes, so that, now that her eyes were closed, nothing remained in the expression of her features but austerity; so that, in addition, the last look I had at her was to remind me, not of her ineffable affec-

---

[5] André Gide often visited the Viscountess de Lestrange at her château of Chitré, near Poitiers.

tion, but of the severe judgment she must have passed on my life.

She used gently to reproach her friend Agnès Copeau [6] for her indulgence. Although she showed considerable herself for the errors and weaknesses of the poor people she succored, she armed herself with unyielding intolerance in regard to those who can find no excuse in poverty for their disorderly life. Not that such severity was natural to her; but what she considered evil it was not sufficient for her to refuse to admit in herself (and her horror of evil was such that this involved no effort), but it even seemed to her that she would have been favoring it by not reproving it most vigorously in others. She held that our society, our culture, our morals were falling to pieces through self-indulgence and a laxity in which she deigned to see only weakness and not liberalism or generosity. Her kindness tempered all that, and what I

---

[6] Agnès Copeau was the Danish-born wife of Jacques Copeau, the creator of the Théâtre du Vieux-Colombier.

9

am saying would surprise those who knew, above
all, the warm glow of her grace. I have met grim
puritans; she resembled them in no way. . . .

No, this is not the way to speak of her appropri-
ately or as I should like to do. Many recollections
immediately rise up in opposition to the portrait
I am trying to draw. It is better simply to remember.

Because she never talked of herself, I know nothing of her earliest personal recollections. She is
present in all of mine. However far back I go, I
see her; or, otherwise, there is nothing but darkness in my early childhood, in which I progress
gropingly. Yet it was only as a result of the tragic
event I recounted in my *Porte étroite* and in *Si le
grain . . .*[7] that she began to play her salutary

[7] The tragic event occurred when André Gide returned un-
expectedly to his cousin's house in Rouen and found her sobbing
over the discovery of her mother's infidelity toward her father.
This marked a turning-point in the lives of both children and
consequently figures prominently in the autobiographic *If It
Die . . .* after having been transposed into the novel, *Strait Is
the Gate.*

role in my life. How old were we then? She fourteen and I twelve, probably. I don't know precisely. But before that I already find her smile in
my past, and it even seems to me that it was only
after being awakened by my love for her that I
became aware of being and really began to exist.
It was enough to make one believe that there was
nothing good in me that did not come from her.
My childish love fused with my first religious fer-
vors; or at least they contained, because of her, a
sort of emulation. Likewise it seemed to me that
by approaching God I was approaching her, and
in that slow ascent I liked to feel the ground, on
both sides of her and me, narrowing.

What would I have been if I had not known
her? I can ask myself this today; but then the
question did not arise. Everywhere I find, thanks
to her, a silver thread in the weave of my thoughts.
But whereas I saw nothing but brightness in hers,
I had to recognize much darkness in me; it was
only the best of me that communed with her.

However great the impulse of my love, it served only, it now seems to me, to divide my nature even more deeply, and I was soon obliged to realize that while aiming to give myself altogether to her (however much I remained a child), that worship in which I held her did not succeed in suppressing all the rest.

Some will be amazed, after what I say, that such an angelic influence did not suffice to preserve from all impurity at least my writings. To our cousin Olga Caillatte, who expressed that sort of amazement, Madeleine told me she had replied: "I don't see that I have any right to influence his thought in the slightest and should be angry with myself if I thought that, out of regard for me, André does not write what he thinks it his duty to write." There were many of my books that she had not read, first because she expressly turned away from any disagreeable or painful object, but also, I believe, through the desire to leave me in this way a greater freedom, a freedom to write without incurring her censure and without fearing to hurt her.

I saw all this without being quite sure of it. Even the most transparent soul keeps many secret recesses hidden, even from the lover. Critical articles and certain insults must have informed Madeleine sufficiently about the nature of some of my writings, even though she had not read them herself. She carefully hid from me the suffering they must have caused her. Rather recently, however, in a letter from her a sentence that seems to contradict what I have just written served as a warning to me: "If you could have known the sorrow that those lines would cause me, you would not have written them." (Yet there was involved here, not what is commonly called morals, but rather a few apparently blasphemous lines that the *Nouvelle Revue Française* had just published and at which she had inadvertently glanced.) [8] It

<hr>

[8] The *Nouvelle Revue Française*, which Gide had founded in 1909 with a group of friends, eventually became the leading

seemed to me that here she was stepping out of her role. . . . No explanation took place between us. I merely overrode this; and her love did likewise.

Trust was natural to her, as to the most loving souls. But to that trust which she brought with her as she came into life fear was soon added. For in regard to anything that was not absolutely genuine she had an extraordinary perspicacity. By a sort of subtle intuition she was warned by an inflection of the voice, by an unfinished gesture, by a trifle; and thus it is that, still very young and the first in her family, she became aware of her mother's misconduct. That painful secret, which at first and for some time she had to keep to herself, marked her, I believe, for life. All her life

monthly literary review of Europe. Probably the passage in question was the journal entry for 6 June 1937, beginning: "Doubtless it is fitting to be suspicious of that illusion (for I really believe it is one) that the last years of a life may be devoted to a more active pursuit of God. . . ." It appeared on the first page of the issue for December 1937, and thus could be read even without cutting the pages of the review.

long she remained like a child who has had a fright. Alas, I was not such as to be able to reassure her much. . . . The little photograph, now half effaced, which shows her to me at the age she then was reveals on her face and in the strangely arched line of her brows a sort of interrogation, of apprehension, of timorous astonishment on the threshold of life. And I felt in myself such joy, such a gushing flood that its overflowing might submerge her sorrow! That is the task I assigned myself and became enamored of. Alas, that superabundance I aimed to share with her was to succeed only in worrying her the more. She seemed to say to me then: "But I don't need so much, for my happiness!"

"My greatest joys I owe to you," she would tell me also; and she would add in an undertone: "and also my greatest sorrows: the best and the most bitter."

But when, today, I reflect on our common past, the sufferings she endured seem to me easily domi-

15

nant, some of them, indeed, so cruel that I am
unable to understand how, loving her as much
as I did, I was not able to shelter her more. But
this is in part because my love involved so much
thoughtlessness and blindness. . . .

I am amazed today at that aberration which led
me to think that the more ethereal my love was,
the more worthy it was of her—for I was so naïve
as never to wonder whether or not she would be
satisfied with an utterly disincarnate love. That
my carnal desires should be addressed to other
objects scarcely worried me at all, therefore. And
I even came to convince myself comfortably that
it was better so. Desires, I thought, belonged to
man; it reassured me not to admit that woman
could experience similar ones unless she were a
woman of "easy virtue." I must confess the out-
rageous fact that such was my heedlessness, which
can be explained or excused only by that ignorance
which life had encouraged in me by offering as
examples only those wonderful feminine figures so-

licitously watching over my childhood: my mother
first, Miss Shackleton, my aunts Claire and Lucile,⁹ models of decorum, respectability, and reserve, to attribute the least carnal perturbation to
whom would have been an insult, it seemed to me.
As for my other aunt, Madeleine's mother, her misconduct had immediately cast her into disrepute,
excluding her from the family, from our horizon,
from our thoughts. Madeleine never spoke of her
and, so far as I know, had never had any indulgence for her; not only through an instinctive protest of her own uprightness, but also in great part,
I suppose, by reason of the sorrow felt by her
father, whom she venerated. That reprobation
contributed to my blindness.

It was not until much later that I began to understand how cruelly I had managed to hurt, to

⁹ Anna Shackleton (*ca.* 1830–84) was a talented Scottish
girl who entered the Rondeaux family in 1850 as tutor to the
seventeen-year-old Juliette (later André Gide's mother) and remained her great friend until death. With her angelic disposi-
tion she deeply influenced Gide's childhood, as did the two
widows Aunt Claire Desmarest and Aunt Lucile.

wound, the one for whom I was ready to give my life—only when, with dreadful thoughtlessness, the most intimate wounds and most painful blows had long been dealt. To tell the truth, my personality could develop only in opposition to her. Indeed, I realized that somewhat; but I did not know that she was very vulnerable. I wanted her happiness, to be sure, but did not think of this: that the happiness to which I wanted to lead and force her would be unbearable to her. Since she seemed to me all soul and, as far as the body was concerned, all fragility, I did not consider that it amounted to depriving her greatly to keep from her a part of me that I counted all the less important because I could not give it to her. . . . Between us no explanation was ever attempted. Never a complaint from her; nothing but mute resignation and an unconfessed rebuff.

I shall tell later on how and by what a strange twist she was subsequently in a position to make me suffer excruciatingly; how neither she nor I

could endure that torture (I am deliberately using a strong word) except through a great effort
to detach ourselves from each other before the
suffering became unbearable . . . before finally
reaching, in the last period, the haven of an understanding for which we had almost ceased hoping.

Doubtless I told myself—and with what remorse!—that she might have liked to be a mother,
but I told myself also that we could never have
agreed about the education of children, and that
other sorrows, other disappointments, would have
been the price she paid for maternity (for I already had an inkling of this from the excessive
concern she had for her sister's children, to whom
she transferred her provision of motherly love).
Nonetheless, those sorrows, those cares, would at
least have been merely normal. I have the remorse
of having warped her destiny.[1]

---

[1] I want to relate here a recollection that seems to me, in
its very discretion, extraordinarily revealing, in regard to both
her and me, of our secret or unconscious reservations:

As I was reading her some pages of my *Immoralist* which

What I fear she was incapable of understanding is that it so happened that the spiritual force of my love inhibited all carnal desire. For I was elsewhere able to prove that I was not incapable of the impulse (I am speaking of the procreative impulse), but only providing that there was no admixture of the intellectual or the sentimental. But how could I have got her to admit that? And probably she modestly attributed that deficiency of my desires to her insufficient charms. Skillful and ever ready to disparage herself, she probably said to herself: "Oh, if only I were more beautiful and knew better how to charm him!" Just to think such a thing is painful to me; but how could it have been otherwise, at least so long as she remained uncertain of the direction of my instincts? How

---

I had just written, she interrupted me at this sentence: "Marceline confessed to me that she was pregnant," and, smiling affectionately, with a touch of roguishness: "But, my dear, it is not a *confesson*," she said; "at most a *confidence*; one *confesses* the reprehensible; *confided to me* is what you want."

[Note supplied by Gide in the French edition. Such notes will hereafter be indicated by an A. in brackets.]

could I have convinced her that of no feminine face, of no look in the eyes, of no smile, of no gesture, of no inflection of the voice, of no grace so much as hers could I have become enamored? For otherwise why so inept in proving this?

I have spoken of my extraordinary sexual ignorance at that age; but my own nature (I mean that of my desires) worried me nonetheless. Shortly before becoming engaged I had therefore made up my mind to unbosom myself to a doctor, a specialist of considerable renown, whom I was rash enough to consult. He smiled as he listened to the confession, which I made as cynically complete as possible; then: "You say, however, that you are in love with a girl and that you are hesitating to marry her, knowing your tastes on the other hand. . . . Get married. Get married without fear. And you will soon see that all the rest exists only in your imagination. You remind me of a starving man who has been trying until now to live on pickles." (I am quoting his words exactly;

21

heaven knows, I remember them well enough!)
"As for the natural instinct, you won't be married
long before you realize what it is and return to it
spontaneously."

What I soon realized, on the contrary, was how
wrong the theoretician was. He was wrong like
all those who insist upon considering homosexual
tastes, when they are found in people who are not
physiologically abnormal, as acquired tendencies
and therefore modifiable through upbringing,
promiscuities, love.

I must note here what I omitted to say in *Si le
grain ne meurt* . . . , but which nonetheless has a
certain importance as refutation of certain theories
which claim to make our sexual tastes depend on
opportunities encountered at a tender age when
instinct, still indecisive, is hesitating and taking
shape. Surrounded as I was, at least during the
summer holidays, by children of my age or slightly
younger, the liberties I took with the boys never
went below the belt; with the girls I indulged in

total indiscretion. Yes, with the boys I maintained a rather marked reserve, in which I believe a keen psychologist might already have seen the very mark of my inclination. Likewise my modesty in the presence of men was excessive, and when my mother, on the advice of our doctor, had decided to have me take showers (I must then have been hardly more than twelve), the very idea of having to stand naked before the bath-attendant made me sick with apprehension. Had the shower been administered by a woman, I believe I should have accepted without any more ado.

Love exalted me, to be sure, but, despite what the doctor had predicted, it in no wise brought about through marriage a normalization of my desires. At most, it got me to observe chastity, in a costly effort that served merely to split me further. Heart and senses pulled me in opposite directions.

MADELEINE

Luxor, 8 February '39 [2]

I open this notebook again after having forsaken
it for several months. Since she ceased to exist, I
have ceased to take much interest in life. Already
I belong to the past. Others enjoy calling it up;
but I wonder if, seeking to revive here the figure
of her who accompanied me in life, I am not going
against her will. For she constantly withdrew,
hiding from attention. Never was she heard to say:
"As for me . . ." Her modesty was as natural as
in other women the need to push oneself forward,
to shine. Even when I would return from a voyage
and the other members of the family would greet
me on the stone steps of Cuverville, I knew that
she would be standing, somewhat withdrawn, in
the shadow of the entrance hall, and I would think
of Coriolanus' return, of the "My gracious silence,

[2] At the end of January 1939 Gide set out alone for Egypt
after correcting the proofs of his *Journal 1889–1939* for the
Pléiade collection. On the last page of that work he noted:
"Nothing recalls me to Paris before May. Here I am free, as I
have never been; frightfully free, shall I still be able to 'try to
live'? . . ."

haill" that he addresses to his Virgilia. . . .[3] When Madeleine burned all my letters, in the tragic circumstances I shall relate, she did so indeed in a gesture of despair and to detach me from her life; but also to escape future attention and through a desire for self-effacement.

It might be thought that such a shrinking was provoked by what seemed to her reprehensible in my life; and, to be sure, it was accentuated by whatever discovery she may have made of that or whatever intuition she may have had; but as far back as I go, I still find such a shrinking. It was constant, natural . . . or, perhaps, already the result of her initial childhood fright, of that first wounding contact with evil, which, on a soul as sensitive as hers was, must have left an indelible bruise. And I already depicted her thus in my first

[3] In Shakespeare's tragedy, Act II, scene i, Coriolanus, on his return home in triumph, notices his wife's silence thus:
My gracious silence, haill
Wouldst thou have laughed had I come coffin'd home,
That weep'st to see me triumph?

books, well before our marriage: Emmanuèle in
the *Cahiers d'André Walter*, Ellis in the *Voyage
d'Urien*. Even the evanescent Angèle of *Paludes*
was somewhat inspired by her. . . .* And in my
dreams she constantly used to appear to me as an
unclaspable, elusive figure; and the dream would
turn into a nightmare. Whence that resolve I
made, when still very young, to do violence to her
reticences and sweep her along with me toward
exuberance and joy. That is where my mistake began.

A double mistake, for at once it made her mis-
judge me even more than I was misjudging her.
Because she was extraordinarily discreet and re-
served, I had to guess almost everything; and often
I was very bad at guessing. Many slight indications might have been revelatory if I had observed
her with sufficient solicitude. I was able to explain

---

* *The Notebooks of André Walter*, an autobiographical
novel of 1891, was Gide's first published work. *Urien's Travels*
(1893) is an allegory, and *Morasses* (1895) the first of his
satires.

them to myself only much later, only too late, and she had let me misinterpret them, for she never defended herself against anything that might offend or harm her. But had I understood earlier, would I have greatly modified my behavior as a result? It is my very nature that I should have had to change—be able to change.

And that she should have been misled in the beginning of our union is natural; but I now believe that that misunderstanding of hers lasted much less long than I then imagined. How could she have failed to begin by suspecting a sensuality of which I gave her so few proofs? Before understanding and admitting that that sensuality was addressed elsewhere, she naïvely expressed surprise that I could have written my *Nourritures terrestres*, a book that she said was so unlike me.[5] Yet even as we descended into Italy after leaving the Engadine during our wedding trip, she was like-

---

[5] *The Fruits of the Earth* (1897) is a lyrical praise of sensation and self-expression.

wise surprised by my animation when the carriage in which we were heading south was escorted by the *ragazzi* of the villages we were going through. Inevitably the connection must have come to her mind, however disagreeable and offensive it may have been for her, so contrary to all the admitted facts and upsetting to the norms on which to establish her life. She felt out of it, brushed aside; loved doubtless, but in what an incomplete way! She did not immediately admit defeat. What, were whatever advances feminine modesty allowed her to remain useless, without echo and without reply? . . . Painfully I can see now the stages of that voyage:

In Florence we visited together churches and museums; but in Rome, completely absorbed by the young models from Saracinesco [6] who then used to come and offer themselves on the stairs

---

[6] Saracinesco is a small village in the province of Rome, supposedly founded in the tenth century by a handful of Saracens and known by the special physical type of its inhabitants, much sought after as artists' models.

of the Piazza di Spagna, I was willing (and here
I cease to understand myself) to forsake her for
long hours at a time, which she filled somehow or
other, probably wandering bewildered through
the city—while, on the pretext of photographing
them, I would take the models to the little apartment we had rented in the Piazza Barberini. She
knew it; I made no secret of it, and if I had, our
indiscreet landlady would have taken care to tell
her. But as a crowning aberration, or else to try to
give to my clandestine occupations a justification,
a semblance of excuse, I would show her the "art"
photographs I had taken—at least the first, altogether unsuccessful ones. I ceased showing them
to her the moment they turned out better; and she
was scarcely interested in seeing them, any more
than she was in going into the artistic considera-
tions that urged me, as I told her, to take them.

Moreover, those photographs soon became nothing more than a pretext, needless to say; little
Luigi, the eldest of the young models, was not at

all misled by them. Any more than Madeleine
herself, probably; and I am inclined to believe
today that of the two of us, the blinder one, the
only blind one, was I. But aside from the fact that
I found it advantageous to suppose a blindness
that permitted my pleasure without too much
remorse, as, after all, neither my heart nor my
mind was involved, it did not seem to me that I
was unfaithful to her in seeking elsewhere a satisfaction of the flesh that I did not know how to ask
of her. Besides, I didn't reason. I acted like an
irresponsible person. A demon inhabited me. It
never possessed me more imperiously than on our
return to Algiers, during the same trip:

The Easter holidays had ended. In the train
taking us from Biskra, three schoolboys, returning
to their *lycée*, occupied the compartment next to
ours, which was almost full. They were but half
clothed, for the heat was tantalizing, and, alone
in their compartment, were raising the roof. I
listened to them laugh and jostle one another. At

each of the frequent but brief stops the train made, by leaning out of the little side window I had lowered, my hand just reached the arm of one of the boys who amused himself by leaning toward me from the next window, laughingly entering into the spirit of the game; and I tasted excruciating delights in touching the downy amber flesh he offered to my caress. My hand, slipping up along his arm, rounded the shoulder. . . . At the next station, one of the two others would have taken his place and the same game would begin again. Then the train would start again. I would sit down, breathless and panting, and pretend to be absorbed by my reading. Madeleine, seated opposite me, said nothing, pretended not to see me, not to know me. . . .

On our arrival in Algiers, the two of us alone in the omnibus that was taking us to the hotel, she finally said to me in a tone in which I felt even more sorrow than censure: "You looked like either a criminal or a madman."

I NEEDED to tell that; but I should like to draw her portrait here rather than to relate our story.

She was afraid of everything, even before being afraid of me; and certainly that fear was increased by the awareness of her fragility. I suggested to her as a motto: *leo est in via* or *latet anguis in herba*.[7] And because a trifle satisfied her and she was happy with very little, she considered as excess everything that went beyond the ordinary. The least wind became a squall to her. She would have needed perpetual calm weather; likewise, an uneventful, smooth-flowing life; especially in recent years, when her greatly impaired health left her heart at the mercy of too great a surprise. But even before she felt so stricken, there was perhaps

~~~~~~~~~~~~

[7] "There is a lion in the way" is from Proverbs, XXVI, 13; "a serpent lies in the grass" is from Virgil's *Bucolics*, III, 93.

not a single action for which I did not have to assume a certain harshness toward her and brace myself to disregard the worry I was causing her. Now, it happened that that worry quickened her love.

I felt this especially when, after the publication of my book on Russia, she thought my life seriously threatened.[8] Likewise, she was brought much closer to me by the attacks I had to undergo, which I bless for that reason. Let me say at once that that reconciliation *in extremis* allowed us to recapture, despite the setbacks and before separating forever, a sort of harmonious felicity as complete as her love deserved. I shall return to this; but first I must speak of the ordeals. . . . Mine came later, just as unbearable as hers had been, to such a degree that each of us in turn made desperate efforts to detach himself from the other: we were suffering too much. It was in religion that she sought refuge—as was natural, for she had

---

[8] His *Return from the U.S.S.R.*, describing his disappointment with the Soviet experiment, came out in 1936.

always been very devout—and in a re-establish-
ment of those bourgeois ideas and practices which
assured her the sort of moral comfort her fragility
so greatly needed.[9] The emancipation to which I
wanted to lead her had made a sorry showing and
could only appear to her as rash and inhuman; in
any case it was not made for her and succeeded
only in wounding her. I tried to bring this out in
my *Immoraliste,* a book that seems to me today
very imperfect, very incomplete at least, for it did
not take into account or scarcely provided a
glimpse of the sharper edge of the sword.

That sword soon turned against me. For she was
not to be satisfied merely with alienating herself
from me; it seemed that she made every effort to
alienate me from her, lopping off from herself little
by little everything that made me love her. Power-
less, I had to watch that sacrilegious mutilation.

[9] To lift her away from her habits would have required
someone in whom she could have complete trust. I behaved so
that she sank back into them, on the contrary, as if hoping to
find in them a protection against me. [A.]

I had cast away the right to intervene, to protest; she made me feel this by disregarding everything I found to say to her; without ever resisting, without deviating from her smiling charm, simply by taking no account whatever of my admonitions. Any arm blunts itself against such gentleness; nothing made any impression. I came to the point of no longer knowing even what I wanted of her; I felt absurd; I was going crazy.

Moreover, even in the best period of our union, she had always "done just what she pleased"; obstinate as women often are even while seeming to yield, offering that resistance of the weak reed that bends before the passing wind and rights itself after the wind has passed. I had never been able to get her to change in the slightest any of her domestic habits; to get her, for instance, to wind the tall clock in the Cuverville hall otherwise than by climbing on a scaffolding of empty boxes, fragile and badly balanced, obstinately refusing the stepladder I used to bring her; at most she

35

would use it in my presence and on that day, but I would notice the following day that the stepladder had resumed its appointed place in the pantry, and when the time came to wind the clock again, the dangerous scaffolding would reappear. And so for the rest; and so for everything. As she used every object awkwardly and rashly, I was constantly on tenterhooks. She would declare inconvenient any instrument of which she did not quite understand the functioning; and when one wanted to show her the best way of going about it, she would assume such a weary and absent-minded look that one would soon give up. At Saint-Moritz, the first stop on our wedding trip, I had taken her with me on a rather long mountain climb that obliged us to spend the night in a shelter before going over the Diavolezza Pass. The pass had nothing exactly dangerous about it, but all the same we were roped together, preceded and followed by guides; we had in hand the stick that is called alpenstock, which she was using for the first time. When it was necessary to cross a rather long space of steep slope covered with snow, the guides and I made useless efforts to get her to hold the alpenstock properly. I feared that at any moment the guides might refuse to go any farther, for in the most dangerous stretch she insisted on holding the stick out over the void, thus running the risk of pulling herself that way and causing her, and all of us, to fall. She protested that that was the way she felt she had to hold it, whereas the other way she did not feel safe. Nothing to be done about it; she wouldn't give up her point! This gave me a nightmare for many nights, and for long afterward. It was the same with everything.

That lopping off of branches of which I spoke above did not begin until later, and the effort to detach me from her after detaching herself from me. I emphasized this in my *Porte étroite*,[1]

---

[1] Indeed, the novel, *Strait Is the Gate*, in which Alissa deliberately makes herself less attractive, was first published in 1909.

anticipating, by some kind of foresight, what reality came to confirm later on. There I related as best I could the effort to "withdraw to her minima," as Barrès would have said.[2] The dreadful thing is that I came to believe (and she strained her ingenuity to force me to believe) that she was not capable of a more complete flowering, that the most exquisite part of all I cherished in her existed only in my imagination, that the real person she was fell far short of my dream. . . . The truth is that she believed I had ceased to love her. Consequently what was the use of embellishing herself to please me? As for pleasing me, there was no longer any point in thinking of it. Thenceforth what did culture, music, poetry matter? She deserted the paths on which she might have run the risk of encountering me; she sank into devotion. I was welcome to be jealous of God or to follow

[2] Maurice Barrès (1862–1923) used this expression in preaching a return to regionalism. See *The Journals of André Gide*, Vol. IV, p. 47.

her onto that mystic ground, the only one where she was still willing for me to communicate with her. She confined herself to it narrowly.

Everything I am saying of this remains abstract if I do not illustrate it with an example. In her youth she had had the most delicate, the prettiest hands one could see; they were expressive and I loved them as if in and for themselves. . . . It seemed as if she soon enjoyed deforming them. There was no coarse work she did not impose on them, seeming to enjoy mistreating them in tasks at which, furthermore, she revealed herself to be very clumsy. If I happened to protest when I surprised her in the pantry busy washing the dishes, she would protest in return that she was simply doing so exceptionally, to relieve the maid, who was busy elsewhere, or would find some expedient or other in an effort to hide from me the fact that she indulged in this work every day. In order to calm me, she would add, moreover, that she took great care of her hands and that while washing the dishes she was careful not to scald them, using only the tips of her fingers. . . . What else can I say? Supplications, objurgations, nothing was of any avail; but if I continued to insist, suddenly her face expressed a mortal fatigue, the outward sign of her resigned obstinacy; and I do not recall a single case in which I did not have to beat a retreat. Knowing her to be otherwise very reasonable, I then looked for some secret reason that she might prefer not to give; I came to think that perhaps she wanted to put herself on an equal footing with her sisters, each one of whom could afford the help of a servant only in the morning. That is what I wondered, for I knew how she suffered from the knowledge that Jeanne and Valentine were less well off than she.[3] But even more I am inclined to believe that she carried humility to the point

---

[3] Jeanne Rondeaux married Marcel Drouin (1871–1943), a professor of philosophy in *lycées* of Alençon, Bordeaux, and Paris. Valentine Rondeaux, the youngest sister, married Marcel Gilbert, who died in 1907.

of no longer allowing herself anything but inferior occupations.

She was two years older than I; but the difference in age, from her appearance on certain days, seemed to be that between two generations. I remember a ride we took to Fécamp.[4] I was counting on great delight from a little time spent alone with her; but she consented to that interruption in her trifling daily occupations only on condition that we take along the two maids, "who will enjoy the ride even more than I," she said. For the happiness of others always came before her own. I was well aware, during the whole drive, that she pretended to enjoy it in order not to sadden me, and that she was probably sensitive to the beauty of the surrounding nature, to the soft, profuse light on the opulence of the wheat fields, but also that she never ceased thinking of all she ought to have done at Cuverville and accepting that dis-

[4] Fécamp is on the Channel coast about seven miles northeast of Cuverville.

traction only for the sake of not detracting from
my joy. At Fécamp I had dropped behind to buy
some cigarettes; I recall that before catching up
with her, I first contemplated her some twenty
yards ahead of me, walking between the two
maids, and that she seemed to me so pitifully
aged that I doubted it was she. "What, is that
what remains of you, my dear? That is what you
have made yourself become!" And I tarried behind for fear of not being able to hide from her
the anguish that filled my heart and wanted to
pour forth in tears. Tears of remorse as well, for
I told myself: it is my work! It was entirely up to
me to keep her from forsaking life. Now it is done.
It is too late and I can no longer change anything. . . . Not having the courage to catch up
with her, I let her return to the hotel alone. And
when, a little later, I heard one of the hotel
servants say to me: "Your mother is waiting
for you in the carriage," I was certainly much
more deeply touched than she herself may per-

haps have been to notice that I was taken for her son.

Her need of giving, of preferring the happiness of others to her own, was instinctive and expressed itself naïvely. I had brought back from my trip to the Congo [5] the only object I had been able to find there that seemed to me worthy of her. It was a wallet on which narrow strips of leather wove together their slashes of color in the happiest fashion. At Bangui, among many ordinary objects for sale, I had noticed it at once; it would have been impossible to find another like it. Certainly, at the moment I gave it to her she admired it greatly. But, two days later: "Would you let me give the wallet to your secretary?" (who had been there only for a few days and whom we hardly knew); "I noticed that she considered it pretty and think she would like it."

[5] The account of Gide's year in Africa, from July 1925 to June 1926, is contained in his *Travels in the Congo*.

43

After the war, fleeing society, she never left
Cuverville any more. On what were her days
spent? Her evenings were short, for she got up
before dawn; as soon as she had made her devo-
tions, she would go down to light the kitchen fire
and prepare the work for the young maids she
was forming (in the Pays de Caux the verb *nater*
is used), who would regularly leave her, as soon
as they were trained, to go and get a job in town.
She hardly read any more at all, for lack of time,
she said. Constantly busy, she would hasten with
rapid step from one end to the other of the house
or garden; you would see her pass, smiling but
elusive, and only with great difficulty could I get
her to grant me an hour for a reading often interrupted by one of the maids coming to ask her
help or advice, by farmers, tradesmen, beggars,
and all the poor of the countryside.[6]

[6] She had had the idea, which I greatly encouraged, of
buying up one after another and repairing the dilapidated cot-
tages of the commune, which were falling into ruins and threat-

I wondered if perhaps, unable to enter holy orders and "pronounce vows" as Edi Copeau had just done,[7] whom she probably envied secretly, she had not at least made a vow to limit herself to trifling daily occupations, like that of going to feed the neighborhood dogs and cats in addition to those belonging to the household. She never failed, whatever the weather might be; and every day at the same time there awaited her in the farmyards a multitude of dogs, of cats especially, scabby, mangy, one-eyed, crippled outcasts to which the farmers paid no attention, and which, without her, would surely have died of hunger, incapable of caring for themselves. Thus she would go, awkwardly holding in front of her in her bare hands a huge pan in which the food she had prepared for them was cooling. Her hands

ening to become uninhabitable because the owners, not managing to collect the rent, refused to make the necessary repairs. [A.]

[7] Edi (Edwige) Copeau, the younger daughter of Jacques and Agnès Copeau, entered the Order of Benedictine Missionaries in 1931 at Vanves, with the name of Mère François; she has since been stationed in Madagascar.

being subject to the frost and rain (for I could not even get her to wear gloves), I saw them spoil more day by day, constantly becoming less fit for any but the coarsest tasks, always holding a pen or pencil with greater difficulty. Needless to say, her correspondence suffered as a result; and her friends, not well informed of that discomfort, were amazed that she sometimes went so long without answering their affectionate messages. What worried me also was that her poor hands were also losing their sensitivity; I noticed this from many indications; she would happen to skin them without even being aware of it, and I used to suffer indescribably at seeing her make no effort to avoid contact with sticky or dirty objects; she seemed to prefer to caress sickly animals and I constantly feared that she might infect herself through the chapped spots she got with the first cold spell, took no care of, and consequently kept unhealed all winter. Under such cruel abuse, her poor delicate hands rapidly became formless things, which I could not see without feeling a frightful pang. "You must have had very pretty hands," said the doctor to whom I had taken her.[8]

Nevertheless, she was much concerned about her eyes. For some time I had been unable to understand a progressive whitening of the edge of the iris (it seemed invaded by the cornea) which was gradually modifying the quality of her expression. Then there occurred a retinal embolism. From the consultation we learned that the eye which had not yet been affected was threatened with a cataract. I should have liked her to spare it, and had brought out for her an old family Bible, printed in large characters. But she was accustomed to *her* Bible and to the prayer-book that Edi Copeau had given her before entering orders; I could change nothing.

Moreover, tired of constantly watching over her, of exhausting myself in ever useless objurga-

[8] See *The Journals of André Gide*, Vol. III, p. 171 (1 July 1931). [A. gives a reference to the French edition.]

tions, I had finally resolved to let her do as she wished without commenting further. Yes, I was dreadfully, mortally tired of taking care of her; I was at the end of my strength. The contest was lost; I gave up. Henceforth I would give her a free rein! Besides, I no longer loved her; did not even want to; loving her made me suffer too much. As for all that I had dreamed, all that I associated with her, did it not already belong to the past, to the tomb where it would all eventually end up?

But, oh marvel! It was when I had finally forced myself to so artificial a detachment that she began to draw closer to me—oh, in an almost imperceptible way and without changing anything in her manner of living. I had come to believe that my presence was a burden to her, bothered her; but what bothered her was solely my remonstrances, she gave me to understand (for never was there the slightest *explanation* between us). And slowly, from the very wreckage of our love, a new harmony, as if supernatural or superhuman, took shape. No, I had not ceased loving her. For that matter, since nothing carnal had ever entered into my devotion for her, that devotion was not to let itself be altered by the weathering resulting from time; for that matter, I never loved Madeleine more than aged, stooped, suffering from varicose veins in her legs, which she would let me bandage, almost disabled, at last surrendering to my attentions, sweetly and tenderly grateful.

What is our love made of, then, I used to wonder, if it persists in spite of the crumbling of all the elements that compose it? What is hidden behind the deceptive exterior that I recapture and recognize as the same through the dilapidations? Something immaterial, harmonious, radiant, which must be called soul, but what does the word matter? She believed in immortality; and I am the one who ought to believe in it, for it is she who left me. . . .

Everything I am relating here may seem, I am well aware, formless and scarcely delineated. But it was characteristic of our story not to offer any sharp outlines. It stretches over too long a time, over my whole life; it is a constant, latent, secret, essential drama marked by very few events; never openly declared.

I perceive that I have said almost nothing of her that is not privative, nothing that might explain perhaps the hold she had on my heart and my thoughts. Yet it will not surprise those who knew her best, though it was quite involuntary, for she no more strove to captivate than to dominate. What I experienced in her presence was above all a deep feeling of harmony. It seemed that a glow, radiating from her, made one suavely share the inner peace she had achieved. Everything in her, by her mere presence, invited one to feel happy.

She loved animals, flowers, all natural things; the most modest bouquet delighted her. In vain I would strive to achieve some selection among the plants in our garden; I was sure to find replanted in a little hospital bed all those I had eliminated. She would replant the Christmas trees after they had served their purpose. She could not resign herself to throwing away the spent bulbs of hyacinths or tulips.

In regard to human beings, she was always very circumspect; her judgments were prompt, severe, and relentless. She did not despise, but, as for certain individuals who did not seem to her authentic, she would cease to consider them, to see them. Her extraordinarily delicate ear would discern at once what was not absolutely genuine. I believe that I drew from her the need for sincerity—although, faced with the excesses of mine, she would repeat Claudel's [9] remark: "Better hypocrisy than cynicism"; and this seemed hardly in accord with her loathing for falsehood. But I well understand what she meant thereby, and that there was no inconsistency in it: it was up to God to distinguish the degree of ingenuousness of our acts; the important thing for society was that those acts should conform to laws, traditions, and morals. She held that France was being lost through tolerance, indulgence, and welcoming *the foreign.* In regard to the last, wherever it came from and whatever it might be, she had a distrust, both instinctive and theoretical, which nothing could shake. On events as on people her verdicts were definitive and admitted no appeal; of what she had judged to be bad, she would decide once and for all that "Nothing good can come of it," and according to the deed judged the consequences, whatever might result. Noth-

[9] Paul Claudel (1868–   ), the great Catholic lyric poet and poetic dramatist, was a friend of Gide from 1899 until 1914, though they occasionally corresponded after that.

ing would make her reconsider. Consequently I kept silent about certain important facts of my life, about certain individuals whose very name was never uttered any more, and never was there any mention of what might hurt her; so that the zone of silence extended ever farther between us. But I believe that it was chiefly in my presence that she armed herself with intransigence, partly through fear of letting herself be influenced by her heart, or at least of letting this be seen. Capable of steadfastness but never of harshness, she preserved, despite her being closely tied to those principles, a smiling and grave amenity like that of Goethe's Iphigenia or, even more, of the ancient Antigone. I do not see any figure to which I can better compare her.

At times I think that feeling her to be so extraordinarily different from me was what made me fall in love with her as I did, through that odd attraction which dissimilarity exerts over me. But also I believe that, the better to oppose me, to resist, she emphasized her dissimilarity. Yet however different from me she may have been, it was having known her that made me so often feel like a stranger on this earth, playing the game of life without too much believing in it, for having known through her a less tangible but more genuine reality. My intelligence might well negate that secret reality; with her, I felt it. And in the absence of the pure sound that soul gave forth, it seemed to me thenceforth that I had ceased to hear any but profane sounds, opaque, faint, and desperate.

It was indeed also that utter authenticity that made so difficult, so impossible, any explanation between us. I thought she would interpret better my very silence and that any protestation of love would run the risk of seeming to her deceitful or at very least exaggerated; and that would at once have made me lose the credit that, slowly, month after month and year after year, I felt I was winning back.

Intimate Journal

HERE are the passages of my *Journals* relating to Madeleine which do not figure in the published editions.[1]

15 *September 1916*

I resume this journal, forsaken last June, in a new notebook. I had torn out the last pages; they reflected a dreadful crisis in which Madeleine was involved; or, more exactly, of which Madeleine was the cause. I had written them in a sort of despair, and because, to tell the truth, those pages were addressed to her, I tore them up at her request as soon as she had read them. Or rather, even though she discreetly refrained from asking

---

[1] Solely the passages in italics appeared, occasionally somewhat modified, in the Pléiade edition of 1939. [A.] It was from that edition that the first three volumes of *The Journals of André Gide* were translated; these passages in slightly different form will be found under the same dates there.

*it of me, at least I was too keenly aware of the
relief it would be for her not to suggest it to her
at once. And probably she was grateful to me
for it; but yet, to speak frankly, I regret the loss of
those pages; not so much because I had never
written any like them, nor because they might
have helped me to get out of an unhealthy state
of mind that they sincerely reflected and into
which I am only too inclined to fall again; but because that suppression interrupted my journal at
once and because, deprived of that support, I have
since wallowed in a terrifying intellectual disorder. I have made useless efforts in the other
notebook. I forsake it half filled. In this one, at
least, I shall not be aware of the gap.*

7 October 1916

*A few words from Madeleine plunge me back
into a sort of despair. As at last I had made up my
mind to speak to her of that plan of spending the*

winter at Saint-Clair,[2] "I certainly owe you that,"
she said with an effort of her whole nature, which
at once made her face so sad, so grave, that im-
mediately I thought only of giving up this plan
like so many others, since it costs her so much and
since I should have to buy my convenience at the
price of her happiness—so that it could therefore
no longer be my convenience.

1 June 1917

It is hateful to me to have to hide from her. But
what else can I do? . . . Her disapproval is unbearable to me; and I cannot ask her to approve
what I feel nevertheless that I must do.

"I loathe indiscretion," she told me. And *I*
loathe falsehood even more. It is to be able finally to speak out some day that I restrained myself all life long.

---

[2] Saint-Clair, not far from Hyères (Var) on the south
coast, was the home of the Belgian painter Théo Van Rysselberghe.

21 November 1918 [*]

Madeleine has destroyed all my letters. She has just confessed this to me, and it crushes me. She did it, she told me, just after I left for England. Oh, I am well aware that she must have suffered dreadfully from my departure with Marc; but did she have to take revenge on the past? . . . It is the best of me that disappears; and it will no longer counterbalance the worst. For more than thirty years I had given her (and I still gave her) the best of me, day after day, the moment I was absent even briefly. I feel suddenly ruined. I have no heart for anything. I should have killed myself without effort.

If this loss were even due to some accident, invasion, fire. . . . But that *she* should have done that! . . .

~~~~~~~~~~

[*] In the edition I brought out, my *Journal* stops at the end of October 1918, not to resume until May 1919; again it stops almost at once for a new silence of almost a year. There it is that the following pages, which explain that long silence, should be inserted. [A.]

22

Did she realize that she was suppressing thus the only ark in which my memory, later on, could hope to find refuge? All the best of me I had entrusted to those letters—my heart, my joy, and my varying moods, the way I spent my days. . . . I am suffering as if she had killed our child.

Oh, I will not endure anyone's accusing her. That is the sharpest pang. All night long I felt it tearing my heart.

24

Took aspirin to try to sleep. But the pain wakes me in the middle of the night and I feel as if I am going mad.

"They were my most precious belonging," she told me.

"After you left, when I found myself all alone again in the big house that you were forsaking, with no one on whom to lean, without knowing what to do, what to become . . . I first thought

that nothing remained but to die. Yes, truly, I
thought that my heart was ceasing to beat, that
I was dying. I suffered so much. . . . I burned
your letters in order to do something. Before de-
stroying them I reread them all, one by one. . . ."

Then it was that she added: "They were my
most precious belonging."

If the sacrifice were to be repeated, she would
do it again, I am convinced. Even independently
of any grievance, modesty alone urged her to
this. She could not endure attracting attention
or glances, and was constantly keeping in the
background. She would like her name never to
be uttered anywhere, except by a few friends'
mouths and by those of the poor peasants she
looks after and who call her "Madame Gille";
and above all she would like to suppress her presence from my writings. . . .[4]

---

[4] I am tempted to modify some of these sentences, which
no longer seem to me quite fair, now that I see perhaps a bit
more clearly; but it is better to make such alterations in a com-

I have always respected her modesty, to such a degree that I almost never take occasion to speak of her in my notebooks and that, even now, I stop. Never again will anyone now know what she was for me, what I was for her.

They were not exactly love-letters; I feel repugnant toward effusiveness and she would not have

~~~~~~~~~~

mentary and maintain all the errors of interpretation which I managed to make then, however tainted with self-indulgence they may seem to me today. Everything I wrote then concerning Madeleine's excessive modesty seems to me correct; it is true that she never sought to cut a figure or to make the most of herself. In that need of withdrawing to the background, there was an element of modesty and of Christian unpretentiousness; but I tell myself today that, through love, she would most willingly and joyfully have accepted appearing at my side and being associated with my fate (let us say: with my fame) in the minds of men, if the notoriety she saw me acquire had not seemed to her of such sinister nature. In the lines I then wrote I left out what now seems to me the most important: with all her heart and all her soul she disapproved my conduct and the direction of my thoughts. That is what above all urged her to withdraw from my life. She suffered unspeakably at the thought of having to figure and assume a role, even a secondary one or that of a victim (and she still loved me too much not to suffer doubly in that case) in a drama that she reprobated wholly, in which she would have wished not to be involved at all, and especially not as an accuser.—I return to what I wrote then and, for my shame, give it without changing anything. (Luxor, February '39.) [A.]

endured being praised, so that I most often hid
from her the emotion with which my heart was
brimming. But in them the pattern of my life was
woven before her eyes, little by little and day by
day.[5]

~~~~~~~~~~~~~

[5] I added, with a fatuousness that makes me smile today
but which sprang from my despair: "Perhaps there never was
a more beautiful correspondence." Let it be said more simply
that I had never written and have never written since *similarly*
to anyone; I made a point of faithfully saving for her everything
I could give to her, and as for the rest strove, not being able to
subjugate it, not to make too much of it. . . .

Today, feeling at the end of my life (not so much because
I am done in as because the game is over and already I am
withdrawing from it), I reread without indulgence the journal
pages I then wrote. The despair in which I thought I was being engulfed came especially, doubtless, from the feeling of failure; I compared myself to Œdipus when he suddenly discovers
the lie on which his happiness is built; I suddenly became conscious of the anguish in which my personal happiness kept her,
whom, in spite of all, I loved more than myself; but also, more
surreptitiously, I suffered at knowing that she had reduced to
nothing all of me that seemed to me to most deserve survival.
That correspondence, kept up since our childhood, probably belonged to both of us at once; it seemed to me born of her as
well as of me; it was the fruit of my love for her . . . and for
a week I wept without stopping, unable to exhaust the bitterness
of *our* loss.

It took place at Cuverville; it was a day like all the other
days. I had needed to look up a date for the *Memoirs* I was then
writing and hoped to find a reference in my correspondence
with her. I had asked her for the key to the secretary in her

25 November

Alas, I am now convinced that I warped her
life even more than she may have warped mine.
For, to tell the truth, she did not warp my life;

~~~~~~~~~~~~

room, where my letters were put away. (She never refused me
that key, ordinarily; but I had not yet asked her for it since my
return from England.) Suddenly I saw her become very pale. In
an effort that made her lips tremble, she told me that the drawer
was now empty and that my letters had ceased to exist. . . .

For a solid week I wept; I wept from morning to evening,
seated beside the fireplace of the living-room where our life in
common was spent, and even more at night, after having withdrawn to my room, where I continued to hope that one evening
she would come to me; I wept ceaselessly, without trying to
communicate anything, and always expecting a word, a gesture
from her . . . but she continued to be busy with her trifling
household duties, as if nothing had happened, frequently passing near me, indifferent, and seeming not to see me. Vainly I
hoped that the persistence of my grief would overcome that apparent insensitivity, but it did not; and probably she hoped that
the despair into which she saw me sinking would bring me
back to God; for she would admit of no other outcome. That,
I believe, is what made her refuse me at least the consolation
of her pity, of her affection. But the tears I wept were as if
nonexistent for her so long as they remained profane; what she
was expecting from me, I suppose, was a cry of repentance and
devotion. And the more I wept, the more we became strangers
to each other; I felt this bitterly; and soon I was weeping no
longer over the destruction of my letters, but over us, over her,
over our love. I felt that I had lost her. Everything in me was
collapsing, the past, the present, our future.

I never again really took any zest in life, or at least not until
much later, when I realized that I had recovered her esteem;

and it even seems to me that all the best of me comes from her. My love for her dominated my whole life but suppressed nothing in me; it merely added conflict.

But what a mistake anyone would make who thought that I had sketched her portrait in the Alissa of my *Porte étroite!* There was never anything forced or excessive in her virtue. Doubtless everything in her wished only to blossom forth sweetly and tenderly. . . . It is for that reason that I cannot console myself. At times I feel that she was never afraid of anything but me.

After the conversations I have just had with her, these last three days, conversations broken by dreadful silences and sobs, but serious and without a word of accusation or reproach on either side, it seemed to me that never again could

but, even then, I never really got back into the dance, living only with that indefinable feeling of moving about among appearances—among those appearances which are called reality. (Luxor, February '39.) [A.]

66

I try to live, or at least that I could live only a life of repentance and contrition. I felt finished, ruined, undone. One of her tears weighs more, I told myself, than the ocean of my happiness. Or at least—for what is the good of exaggerating?— I no longer saw that I had any right to buy my happiness at the expense of hers.

But why am I speaking of happiness? It is my life, my very existence that wounds her—what I can suppress but not change. And it is not only the sunlight but the very air that is refused me.

Since all my life seemed meant for fails . . . [e]

11 December

Back from Paris four days ago.

Frightful days. My back is broken and I can no longer lift the weight of yesterday's joy. How

---

[e] Gide quotes in English this line from Browning's *Last Ride Together*.

can I recover that self-confidence which helped me to live? I no longer have any heart for anything, and all the light in my heaven is extinguished.

19 December

I am busy going over and polishing the draft of my *Memoirs* [*Si le grain* . . .] so as to keep a complete text if I give a copy to Verbecke.[7] I am not very satisfied with this rereading: the sentences are soft. It is too conscious, too tense, too literary. . . .

I have gone back to the piano; have taken up the *Well-Tempered Clavichord* again.

I feel closing over me again this too calm life in which I stifle and whence I could escape only with another dreadful wrench. Extreme weakness and aging. Whatever might again make my heart beat rapidly could only be for her a cause of

[7] Verbecke directed the Saint Catherine Press of Bruges, which printed in 1920 and 1921 the first edition of the memoirs entitled *If It Die* . . . in an edition of twelve copies.

suffering and horror. I can assert none of me without wounding her, and solely by suppressing myself could I ensure her happiness.

It always seems to them (and this was the case of Wilde) that it is not as victims to their theories that they succumb, but rather, on the contrary, for having been inconsistent with themselves on some point. Wilde insisted on this at length: it is not for having been an individualist, but for not having been one sufficiently, that I repent today.

· *22 December*

Certain days, certain nights especially, I feel crushed by regret for those annihilated letters. It was in them above all that I hoped to survive.

20 January 1919

. . . That implied a sort of contract, regarding which the other party had not been consulted; a contract that I imposed on her; which I imposed on her, moreover, only because my nature imposed its peremptory conditions on me.

Henceforth my work will merely be like a symphony from which the sweetest chord is lacking, like an unfinished building.[8]

~~~~~~~~~~

[8] Here came a few pages, which in the Pléiade edition of my *Journal*, are classified inadvertently as "Detached Pages" of 1923. (See pp. 777–8.) [A.] This is the passage:

. . . There is a certain indulgence by which every sentiment we experience is exaggerated; and often one does not suffer so much as one imagines oneself to be suffering.

I have never been able to renounce anything; and protecting in me both the best and the worst, I have lived as a man torn asunder. But how can it be explained that this cohabitation of extremes in me led not so much to restlessness and suffering as to a pathetic intensification of the sentiment of existence, of life? The most opposite tendencies never succeeded in making me a tormented person; but made me, rather, perplexed—for torment accompanies a state one longs to get away from, and I did not long to escape what brought into operation all the potentialities of my being. That *state of dialogue* which, for so many others, is almost intolerable became necessary to me. This is also because, for those others, it can only be injurious to action, whereas for me, far from leading to sterility, it invited me to the work of art and immediately preceded creation, led to equilibrium and harmony.

It must, however, be recognized that, for a number of souls which I consider among the best tempered, happiness lies not in comfort and quietude, but in ardor. A sort of magnificent using up is all the more desirable to them because they are constantly being renewed by it and do not so much suffer

Cuverville, 8 October 1919

(Anniversary of my marriage.) I do not know which is more painful: not to be loved any longer, or to see the person you love, and who still loves you, cease to believe in your love. I have been unable to get myself to love her less, and I remain close to her, my heart bleeding, but without speaking. Ah, shall I ever again be able to talk with her? . . . What is the good of protesting that I love her more than anything in the world? She would not believe me. Alas, it is in my power today only to wound her further.

~~~~~~~~~~

from the wearing away as they rejoice in their perpetual re-creation. As for me, I can tell you that I have never so keenly felt myself growing old as in that very quietude to which your rule of conduct invites one, but which you are less likely to achieve the more earnestly and nostalgically you strive to attain it. Your belief in the survival of souls is nourished by the need of that quietude and your *lack of hope* of enjoying it in life.

Shall I tell you what keeps me from believing in eternal life? It is that almost perfect satisfaction I enjoy in effort itself and in the immediate realization of happiness and harmony. (*The Journals of André Gide*, Vol. II, p. 343.)

10 October

Meanwhile life resumes all the fallacious appearance of happiness.

At Cuverville for the past three weeks, I go back to Paris this evening for ten days.

21 November

Worked tolerably all these recent days; but an abominable sorrow submerges me: I have caused the unhappiness of her whom I love most in the world. And she no longer believes in my love.[9]

Cuverville, 3 January 1921

Atrocious days. Insomnia; relapses into the worst; bad work in which, without any fervor whatever, I try to take advantage of a little remaining momentum.

[9] See *The Journals of André Gide*, Vol. II, pp. 258–61. (The author gives a reference to the French edition, here and in similar cases.)

Oh, if only I could believe that my presence here was pleasing to her. . . . But even that joy is denied me; and all day long I can think only that she merely tolerates me. Nothing of me interests her any more or matters to her; and, as it always takes love to understand what differs from you, I feel nothing in her toward me but incomprehension, misjudging, or, what is worse, indifference.

And yet, at times, I wonder if I am not also making a mistake. Ah, if only we could talk it over! But the least words issue so painfully from my heart that I no longer know how to talk to her.

. . . Her very voice, her sweet voice that I loved as much as anything in this world, her dear voice is no longer the same. The little accident caused last summer by her awkwardness or lack of caution, which first seemed to us of little importance, causes a sort of very slight, almost imperceptible hissing—which I am the only one to notice (her sisters maintain that I am imagining it). Probably this involves nothing that she could not correct, if only she were willing to pay some attention to it; and what especially saddens me is seeing in this forsaking, this renunciation of her charm that she has no further desire to please me and that she has said once for all: what is the use? It even seems that she is trying to give me weapons against her and striving to make me lose interest in her, to invite me to leave her; but all this makes me love her even more, especially since I can express none of it.[1]

~~~~~~~~~~

[1] That was indeed the most tragic part of it: that frightful silence during those long days, those long successions of days which we lived in each other's company. And this is also, often at the limit of my endurance and feeling my love agonizing in that silence, what made me entrust at least to my *Journal*, in these pages I am transcribing, what I could not manage to tell her (through great need, and also through hope, if I happened to die before her, of leaving some evidence of that love which she doubted. I thought that, by chance, she would come to know it and would let herself be convinced by these lines, not addressed to her, better than by what I might have said to her). As for her, I do not believe she ever confided anything of her own torments to anyone; to God alone; and her piety was increased thereby. [A.]

If only I were permitted the hope of bringing her a little happiness. . . .

5 January

The fragment of my memoirs in the December issue of the *N.R.F.* does not have the pages cut. On the other hand she has read Claudel's *Saint Martin*; but probably the last page of my memoirs, which faces the beginning of the *Saint Martin* (it is enough for her to have caught a glimpse of a few lines), put her on her guard; she probably took fright and, according to her custom, refused to look further.[2] So that, doubtless, she now believes that I immodestly flaunted what, on the contrary, I took such great care to hide—even though the whole account suffers as a result.

[2] The last page of Gide's memoirs in the *N.R.F.* for December 1920 concerns the moment in childhood when Abel Vautier showed Gide his precious letters from his sister and then asked for Gide's secrets, which the boy refused to share with another because they could only have related to his cousin Madeleine.

6 January

With despair he realizes that it was only through love for him that she interested herself in those things (art, music, poetry) which for him remain the supreme occupation of his life. She ceased to take pleasure in them and to believe in them at the same time that she ceased to love him.[3]

26 January 1921

I am leaving Cuverville tomorrow. The physiological and moral conditions in which I find myself here are most depressing, and my work has suffered considerably therefrom. I no longer savor here even the joy of making her happy; that is to say that I no longer have that illusion; and the

~~~~~~~~~~~~~

[3] I was right to write the above lines in the third person, as if to disown that thought or at least to detach it from me. It would have been truer to say that, eager to free herself from her love for me, she forbade herself any domain in which I had first accompanied her and where she feared still to encounter me. There was also in her a constant need to impoverish herself. [A.] See *The Journals of André Gide*, Vol. II, pp. 262–3.

thought of that failure haunts my nights. I even
come to the point of thinking that my love is a
burden to her; and at times I reproach myself with
that love as a weakness, as a madness, and try to
force myself to stop suffering from it. . . . I cannot reconcile myself to the divorce of our minds.
She is the only one I love in the world, and I really
cannot love anyone but her. I cannot live without
her love. I accept having the whole world against
me, but not her. And I must hide all this from her.
I must play with her, and like her, a comedy of
happiness.

Paris, 15 May

. . . .

Madeleine announces her arrival for Tuesday. I
was already expecting her Thursday; then Friday,
and I went to meet her at the station. The idea
that she is going to travel the day after a holiday
and in a crowded train keeps me in a state of con-
tinual anguish. My love for her is as much a part of

my life as ever, and I can no more tear it out of my heart than I can tear desire out of my flesh. . . .

Monday, 29 May

She leaves me at four o'clock. I take her to the train at Saint-Lazare.

At moments, despite the strange puffiness that fatigue so often gives her features, I recovered her face—her smile, her expression—which is what I have most loved in the world.

18 July

It seems to me that I desire everything less keenly since that felicity is less accessible that I promised myself from perfect communion with her.

Cuverville, 12 October '21

. . . .

I manage to protect my tranquillity, to maintain my even temper, and to preserve some interest in work, in life itself, only by turning my attention

away from her, from her situation, from our rela-
tionship. If I happen to think of this at night, it
is all up with my sleep and I wallow in an abyss
of anguish and despair. At such times I feel that
I love her as much as ever and suffer frightfully at
not being able to communicate this to her. The
attitude she imposes on me, this mask of indifference that she forces me to put on, certainly seems
to her more sincere than what I could but stam-
mer. She is satisfied with it; and I have no right to
disturb the calm it gives her. In order to maintain
that calm, she needs to believe that I have ceased
loving her, that I never loved her much; only thus,
doubtless, can she preserve a sort of apathy toward me.

.   .   .   .

12 December [*]

.   .   .   .

What can I do? What can I become? Where
can I go? I cannot cease loving her. Her face on

[*] See *The Journals of André Gide*, Vol. II, p. 279.

certain days, the angelic expression of her smile, still fill my heart with ecstasy, love, and despair. Despair at being unable to tell her. Not a single day, not a single moment, have I dared speak to her. Both of us remain walled up in our silence. And occasionally I tell myself that it is better so and that anything I could say to her would merely bring on other sufferings.

I cannot imagine myself without her; it seems to me that without her I should never have been *anything*. Each of my thoughts sprang into being in relation to her. For whom else should I have felt such an urgent need to explain myself? And what gave such power to my thoughts if it were not the "despite so much love"?

. . . .

3 January 22

. . . .

Madeleine writes me: "I am greatly worried by the campaign of vilification opened up against you.

Of course it is the force of your thought and its au-
thority that has instigated this. Oh, if only you
were invulnerable, I should not tremble. But you
are vulnerable, and you know it, and I know it."

Vulnerable . . . I am so, I was so, only through
her. Since, it is all the same to me and I have ceased
fearing anything. . . . What have I to lose that is
still dear to me?

Carry-le-Rouet, 7 August 1922 [5]

A letter from her. A simple little sentence an-
nouncing that she has given to her godchild Sabine Schlumberger the gold necklace and little
emerald cross she used to wear cuts me like a
knife. I cannot endure the idea that anyone else
should wear that cross, which I attributed to
Alissa. . . . What can I reply? She has ceased believing in my love and does not want to know
about my heart. In order to detach herself from

[5] See *The Journals of André Gide*, Vol. II, p. 308.

me more easily, she needs to believe in my indifference. I doubt if I have ever loved her more,
and hate myself for having had to make her suffer,
for having to make her suffer still. I no longer cling
to anything; I often feel so detached from everything that it seems to me I am already dead and
was living only through her.

. . . .

Colpach, 10 September *
Hateful days of idleness and listlessness. . . .
Each morning I wake up with my brain heavy and
more numbed than the day before. Forced, in the
presence of others, to play a comedy of joy and
pleasure—while I feel all real joy slowly cooling in
my heart.

I have received no further letters from her since

* Mme Mayrisch de Saint-Hubert made her château of
Colpach in Luxemburg a meeting-place of French and German
cultures by gathering poets, philosophers, painters, and sculp-
tors as her guests.

82

Pontigny—nay, since Carry-le-Rouet, it seems to me.⁷ In other words, not the slightest sign of life from her since the letter in which she announced the gift of her little emerald cross to Sabine. Does she hold a grudge against me for the reproaches contained in the letter I wrote her in return? Did she resolve not to write me any more? Or does she lack the courage? . . . I feel forsaken by her. Everything good, generous, pure that she aroused in me relapses, and that abominable ebbing draws me down toward hell. Often I wonder, as I did at Llanberis, whether she is not secretly and mystically warned, by some exquisite intuition, of all I do at a distance from her, or at least of whatever might hurt her the most. Did she not give away her necklace the very day when, on the beach at Hyères, Elisabeth came to join me (16 July)? Nothing since. My heart is full of darkness and

⁷ Gide had spent the ten days from the 14th to the 24th of August at the abandoned Abbey of Pontigny, where Paul Desjardins regularly organized summer discussion groups.

tears. I take a dislike to all those here, and everything separating me from her which justifies her tearing herself away from me.

When I thought this morning of how little I am worth without her, when I gauged the scant virtue in my heart, I came to the point of appreciating the necessity for intermediaries between man and God, for those intercessors against whom Protestantism so violently revolts. And I likewise come to appreciate the demon's intricate game and how the noblest sentiments are those he most envies and strives to turn back against God. . . . I don't know whether anything of me subsists on which still to base any hope.

. . . .

31 October

She constantly acts toward me as if I no longer loved her; and I act toward her as if she still loved me. . . . At times it is frightfully painful.

Saint-Martin-Vésubie, 11 July 23 [8]

I have never wanted anything but *her* love, *her* approval, *her* esteem: And since she has withdrawn all that from me, I have lived in a sort of infamy in which good has lost its reward and evil its ugliness, even pain its sting. A sort of numbness of my soul is matched by a softening of everything, and nothing sharp ever penetrates me any more, or rather nothing really penetrates me. Reality touches me hardly any more than would a dream. It often seems to me that I have already ceased living. This is because with her I felt all interest in life withdraw from me; this is because henceforth I care about nothing and no longer value anything.

.   .   .   .

[8] See *The Journals of André Gide*, Vol. II, p. 332. Saint-Martin-Vésubie is in the Alpes-Maritimes.

MADELEINE

Beginning of January 1925[*]

I must admit that my suffering at Cuverville
three years ago was much greater than any I
should have upon leaving life today. Did Madeleine realize this? I do not think so. I fear she may
have seen some exaggeration in my tears. . . .
That is why, since then, I have never been able to
talk with her.

Madeleine might have believed that that suffering (supposing it seemed sincere to her) would
regenerate me; but really, during those dreadful
days, I ceased living; then it was that I took leave.

Since then I have lived only a sort of posthumous
life, as if on the fringe of real life.

"Nothing good can come from that," she frequently said to me, as if to try to persuade herself
of this. It is not true. It is on the contrary from that

~~~~~~~~~

[*] From the little notebook I took to the hospital where I
was operated on for appendicitis. [A.] The operation apparently
took place in the last days of December 1924.

dreadful judgment that came all the bitterness in my life.

Abominable.

I have not ceased loving her, even at the periods when I seemed, and when she had a right to think me, farthest from her—loving her more than myself, more than life itself; but I was no longer able to tell her this. . . .

My entire work is inclined toward her.

At times I could think that, suspecting this, and in order to allow my thought greater freedom, she tried to detach me from her as to detach herself from me; to give me again, and at the same time to recover herself, a lost freedom.

Until *Les Faux-Monnayeurs* (the first book I wrote while trying not to take her into account [1]), I

---

[1] Elsewhere Gide tells that he wrote *The Counterfeiters* for Marc Allégret (*The Journals of André Gide,* Vol. III, p. 15).

wrote everything to convince her, to win her esteem. It is all only a long plea for the defense; no
work has been more intimately motivated than
mine—and no one is very farsighted who fails to
distinguish this.

February 1925

. . . I should like Agnès, then, to whom she
listens, to tell her and make her realize—if I were
not to return from this voyage to the Congo [2]—
that she was the dearest thing to me in the world
and that it was because I loved her more than life
itself that, after she had withdrawn from me, life
seemed to me of so little value.

Cuverville, 14 June '26

*I feel again that odd numbness of the mind, of
the will, of my whole being, which I rarely experience except at Cuverville. Writing the least note*

---

[2] My voyage to the Congo was put off until 14 July '25,
and this allowed me to finish *The Counterfeiters.* [A.]

takes an hour; the least letter, a whole morning. I hang on here only out of love for her, with the painful feeling that I am sacrificing my work, my life, to her. What can I do about it? I can neither leave her nor get her to leave Cuverville, the only refuge on earth to which any roots still bind her, where she does not feel too much in exile. . . .

I was still full of fervor just a few days ago; it seemed to me that I could move mountains; today I am crushed.

. . . .

1 July 1926
The slow progress of Catholicism on her soul; it seems to me that I am watching the spreading of a gangrene.

Every time I come back after having left her some time, I find new regions affected, deeper, more secret regions, forever incurable. And if I could, would I attempt to cure her? That health *which I would offer her, mightn't it be mortal to her? Any effort exhausts her.*

What a convenience, what a rest, what a minimum of effort is offered her by that carefully dosed piety, that fixed-price menu for souls that cannot spend much!

Who could have believed it?—Could God himself have expected it? What! everything that attached me to her, that rather vagabond mood, that fervor, that curiosity, all that did not really belong to her, then? What! it was only out of love for me that she clothed herself in it? All that comes undone, falls off, reveals the bare soul, unrecognizable and fleshless.

And everything that constitutes my raison d'être, my life, becomes foreign and hostile to her.

13 February 1927

"The approbation of a single mere respectable man," she told me, "is the only thing that matters

to me, and that your book will not get." But whoever approves my book ceases to appear respectable in her eyes.

Likewise, before some of the most important acts
of my life she would write me: "Nothing good can
come of it," and consequently would refuse to recognize as good anything that might ensue.—These
are final judgments.

Heidelberg, 12 May 1927

The game is lost, which I could win only with
her. Lack of confidence on her part, and great as-
sumption on mine. It is no good to recriminate, or
even to regret. What is not is what could not be.
Whoever starts out toward the unknown must con-
sent to venture alone. Creusa, Eurydice, Ariadne,
always a woman tarries, worries, fears to let go and
to see the thread break that ties her to her past.
She pulls Theseus back and makes Orpheus look
back. She is afraid.

91

MADELEINE

Paris, 21 August 1938 [3]

Finding myself quite alone and with almost no work to do, I decide to begin this notebook, which, for several months, I have been carrying with me from one halting-place to another with the desire to write in it anything but this; but since Madeleine left me I have lost the taste for life and, consequently, ceased to keep a journal that could have reflected nothing but disorder, distress, and despair.

. . . .

Since she has ceased to exist, I have merely pretended to live, without taking any further interest in anything or in myself, without appetite, without taste, or curiosity, or desire, and in a disenchanted universe; with no further hope than to leave it.

All the work of my mind, these recent months, was a work of negation. And not only did I put my value in the past, but that past value seemed to me imaginary and not worth the least effort to re-

[3] Mme André Gide died at Cuverville on 17 April 1938.

capture it. I was, I still am, like someone sinking into a noisome morass, looking all around him for anything whatever that is fixed and solid of which to catch hold, but dragging with him and pulling into that muddy inferno everything he clutches. What is the good of speaking of that? Unless, perhaps, so that someone else, desperate like me, will feel less alone in his distress when he reads me; I should like to hold out a helping hand to him.

Will I get out of this quagmire? I have already gone through periods of opprobrium when the apostle's cry sprang to my heart: "Lord, save us: we perish!" (And I even knew how to utter this cry in Greek.) For it did not seem to me that any salvation was possible without some supernatural intervention. And yet I got out of it. But I was younger. What does life still hold in store for me?

I cling to this notebook, as I have often done: as a system. A system that used to work. The effort attempted in this way seems to me comparable to that of Baron Munchausen tearing himself from the morass by pulling himself by the hair. (I must already have had recourse to this image.) The wonderful thing is that he manages to do so.

26th in the evening

What does not seem to me quite fair, on the other hand, is holding my grief responsible for my languid condition; it is my grief that led me to it; it is not especially that which keeps me in it. And I am probably not in very good faith when I convince myself of it. I find in it a too easy excuse for my cowardice, a cover for my laziness. I was expecting that grief, I foresaw it for a long time, and yet I imagined my old age, in spite of grief, only as smiling. If I cannot succeed in attaining serenity again, my philosophy is bankrupt. To be sure, I have lost that "witness of my life" who committed me not to live "negligently" as Pliny said to Montaigne, and I do not share Madeleine's belief in an

94

*afterlife which would lead me to feel her eyes upon
me beyond death; but, just as I did not allow her
love, during her life, to influence my thought in her
direction, I must not, now that she is no longer, let
weigh upon my thought, more than her love itself,
the memory of that love. The last act of the comedy
is no less good because I must play it alone. I must
not sidestep it.*

. . . .

Marseille, 26 January '39
*Before leaving Paris, I was able to finish going
over the proofs of my* Journal.⁴ *Upon rereading it,
it seems to me that the systematic suppression (at
least until my loss) of all the passages relative to
Madeleine have, so to speak, blinded it. The few*

---

⁴ The Pléiade edition of the *Journal* covering the years
1889–1939 was published in Paris during the summer of 1939.
The first three translated volumes of *The Journals of André
Gide* correspond to that edition.

allusions to the secret drama of my life become incomprehensible through the absence of what would throw light on them; incomprehensible or inadmissible, the image of that mutilated me that I give there, which presents, in the ardent place of the heart, but a hole.

Paris, 17 April 1928 [1]

DEAR SIR:

I read your letter with the most attentive interest but am sorely embarrassed to reply.

You may be sure that in psychology there are nothing but individual cases and that, in a case like yours, too hasty generalizations may lead to the most serious errors.

With this reservation, allow me to consider as most unwise a matrimonial experiment which, if it fails, will surely compromise a woman's happiness and very probably yours as well if your heart is in the right place. But let me repeat that all cases are individual, and in order to advise you pertinently, it would not suffice for me to know you better; I should also have to know her to whom you would be attaching yourself.

The question of a confession is as ticklish as can

---

[1] The translator has added to this edition this letter to an unidentified correspondent which appears in Vol. XV of the *Complete Works of André Gide.*

be. I am tempted to tell you: if you do not make one immediately (I mean before the marriage), never make it. But in that case arrange yourself so as never to have to make one—and you will surely need to make one sooner or later if you are not capable of behaving as a husband.

As a general rule, it is better to sacrifice oneself than to sacrifice another person to oneself. But all that is theory; in practice it happens that one becomes aware of the sacrifice only long after it is accomplished.

Farewell, sir. To this semblance of advice I add my best wishes and beg you to believe them most sincere.

ANDRÉ GIDE